Dogs have a way of capturing the hearts and attention of children, which is why I've made Maude the primary teacher in this book. Dogs are loyal and devoted, and many of them are filled with unconditional love. They provide comfort and companionship.

In this story, Addie learns a mindfulness practice that is taught by both Maude and Addie's Grammy, including lessons of sensory awareness, as well as relational awareness between humans and their beloved pets.

Creating space and time for bonding is critical for coping with the ever-present, demanding expectations that both children and adults face daily. Grammy creates the first Mindfulness Day, where electronics are left at home during their walk and time exploring. Savoring the present moment is the primary objective.

In this time of electronics and crowded schedules, I believe we need to return to a calmer, slower pace of life for ourselves and for the little ones we love. This book is an opportunity to show adults and children how to slow down and savor the moments of a morning routine, a routine that includes the first bathroom break of the day, stretching and waking up, picking out clothes to wear, and eating breakfast.

As a little girl, my own dog, Fluffy, was by my side constantly. We would walk in the woods together or just sit in the Pampas grass and watch the world go by. We watched clouds, rabbits, and squirrels, and felt the breezy mountain air.

We also slept together, and Fluffy would sit outside my bathroom door, waiting for me to emerge, or stay under the kitchen table looking for opportunities to snag a morsel of food.

Fluffy and I learned mindfulness before I even knew what it was.

However you choose to use *Mindful Moments with Maude*, enjoy it and encourage the children in your life to pay attention to life's cherished moments filled with awareness and connection.

–Pamela Cappetta, EdD

www.mascotbooks.com

Mindful Moments with Maude

For more information, please contact:
Mascot Books
620 Herndon Parkway, Suite 320
Herndon, VA 20170
info@mascotbooks.com

Library of Congress Control Number: 2021913035

CPSIA Code: PRT1221A
ISBN-13: 978-1-63755-377-0

Printed in the United States

Mindful Moments with Maude

Pamela Cappetta, EdD

Illustrated by David Gnass

"Morning, Maude," Addie said sleepily. As she spoke, she slowly remembered the thunderstorm overnight.

"That storm was so loud, Maude, but I wasn't scared," Addie said, trying to believe her own fib.

"You were very brave," Maude yawned. "But I jumped up on the bed anyway to make sure you knew I was right here."

Addie leaned over and looked deeply into Maude's big, brown eyes. "Visiting Grammy is the best thing ever, Maudie. I get to play with you and PJ, too!"

"We love it when you come to visit," said Maude with a big stretch. "Maybe we can have a peaceful day today after such a loud night."

"Maude, how did you stay so calm last night?"

"Well, when I was a puppy, I was afraid of thunderstorms. I would jump on Grammy's bed. She taught me to notice my body and focus on my breath. I can teach you if you want."

"Try to notice simple things when you wake up," said Maude. "Raise your arms above your head, and put your feet on the floor beside your bed. Now breathe... Feel your breath as it moves in and out of your body. How do you feel? I bet you're surprised that it takes so much energy to wake up in the morning."

"Maybe I'll just go back to sleep!" Addie teased.

Maude padded after Addie into the bathroom. "Stop and think," she said. "What do you notice about your body this morning?"

Addie thought for a minute.

"My tummy feels full. I need to go to the potty—right now!"

"Maude, hear that sound in the potty?" asked Addie. "It tinkles. Now my tummy feels soft."

"Soft is good!" said Maude, wiggling her tail.

After brushing her teeth, Addie went back to her bedroom to have some quiet time with Maude before breakfast.

"Let's sit for five minutes and just do some breathing," Maude said.

"Maude... I know how to breathe!" replied Addie, rolling her eyes.

"But this is mindful breathing. Come on, try it. You'll see. This is what Grammy taught me."

Maude climbed onto the blankets. She circled around, scratched a few times, and then settled down.

"You look funny, Maude." Addie giggled. "Like you're chasing your tail."

"It's good to get comfy before you do your breathing," said Maude. "First, find a cozy spot. Lean against the window till your back is straight. Then pay attention to your breath. Now just breathe in, through your nose or your mouth. Then breathe out. Breathe in again, counting to 3 as you breathe: 1... 2... 3. Now breathe out, and count to 3 again: 1... 2... 3. It's easy."

"Notice anything?" Maude asked.

"I kept thinking about things, like the storm noises, putting chocolate chips in my pancakes, going to the lake, my favorite flip-flops... everything but breathing."

"That's okay," said Maude. "It's normal for your mind to wander a bit. Just come back to your breath as soon as you realize you're thinking about something else. Feel the breath as your tummy goes up and down. Try it now one more time. Breathe in: 1... 2... 3. Breathe out: 1... 2... 3."

Addie followed the counting as Maude cocked her head and watched.

"Awesome, Addie! Do you like breathing through your nose or your mouth best?"

"My nose, I guess."

"Either one's okay. Just pick what you like right now, today. Does your breath feel warm or cool?"

"Warm."

"When you breathe in or out, can you feel your tummy move?"

Addie nodded yes.

"Good morning, you two. I hope you slept well," Grammy said. "The storm was really loud last night. Maude, did you protect Addie?"

"She sure did, Grammy! She's teaching me to notice my breath to calm myself down and to feel my body. She says it's okay to slow down and stop rushing."

"She's teaching you to be mindful—to notice little things, like how her cool nose feels when it touches my warm one," Grammy said, touching Maude's nose with her own.

"Go ahead now, while I finish making breakfast. Have fun."

After Grammy left, Addie began getting dressed. "What's that mean, learning to be mindful, Maudie?" she asked.

"Mindful is a funny word, isn't it? It means paying attention to things—how they look or smell or feel, right now. Like how bright the sun is, or how clouds get gray sometimes before it rains. Those kinds of things."

"Like how birds sing in the morning, or how Grammy's marigolds make me sneeze!" said Addie. "I mean really big Ah-Ah-Achooos!"

Addie rummaged through the play clothes in her drawers. "Maude, should I wear orange shorts with a flowered green t-shirt?"

"I'm not so good with clothes," Maude said, tilting her head to one side. "But use mindfulness. Touch them; how do they feel?"

"Ooh, they're very soft," Addie answered, touching the fabric to her cheek. "I like that. Scratchy stuff makes me itch."

(Maude's eyes got big. She wanted to scratch behind one ear just thinking about it!)

Addie held the clean shorts against her nose and breathed in. "They smell like... lavender shampoo. That's my favorite!"

Addie stopped and thought for a minute. "This is being mindful, Maude. I get it!"

Maude stood up and shook her body from head to tail till her collar jingled. "Good job, Addie," she said. "And when we get downstairs, you can pay attention to how the pancakes taste."

"I need to make the bed," said Addie, pulling up her comforter. "And I'm hungry. Come on, Maude. Let's go get breakfast!"

Maude padded behind Addie out the door. "Okay, but we're eating mindfully!"

Addie grabbed some flip-flops and followed Maude into the hallway. But at the top of the stairs, the big dog stopped.

"Addie, try to feel your feet while you're walking downstairs to the kitchen."

"How do I do that?" she asked. "I can't reach over and touch my toes while I'm walking down the stairs."

"Use your imagination," said Maude. "Notice how your feet feel when you touch the steps."

Addie held on to the railing while Maude ambled beside her. The young girl noticed how her hand felt gliding down the wooden rail.

"The wood feels smooth," Addie said thoughtfully. "My feet bend so e-a-s-i-l-y. And the carpet tickles my toes!"

Addie took Maude out for a quick potty break before breakfast.

"Look, Maude. Marigolds!" said Addie. "Uh, oh. Ah... Ah... ACHOO! They're pretty, though," she said, scrunching up her nose.

"You're doing it, Addie—you're being mindful! You're naming things that catch your attention. Noticing simple things is what it's all about."

"Well, now I'm noticing that I'm really hungry. Let's eat!"

Addie gave Maude a little pat on her nose before heading indoors. "Thanks for teaching me this, Maudie. I love you!"

Grammy reminded Addie to wash her hands before breakfast.

Before Addie knew it, Maude sat down on her back legs by the kitchen sink, lifted her front paws up in the air, and barked. "Woof!"

Addie pretended to rub soap on Maude's paws. Then she washed her own hands. "Grammy, this soap's really creamy," she called out. "And I like how it smells!"

Maude took a whiff.

"It's lemony!" Addie added.

"I see Maude's teaching you a lot about mindfulness," Grammy said, tossing her granddaughter a kitchen towel.

For breakfast, Addie had an egg and two pancakes: one with blueberries, and the other with chocolate chips. And they were so good that she smacked her lips!

"Addie, slow down a little," said Grammy. "Chew slowly, and pay attention to every bite. How do the pancakes taste in your mouth?"

"I like that the chocolate chips are so gooey and chocolatey. Some of them melt on my tongue. The blueberries are tart."

Addie savored every bite and grinned from ear to ear. "Thank you, Grammy! I love you."

After breakfast, Addie put dishes in the sink and asked to play on her computer tablet.

"Let's have one day without a computer or a tablet, or even a phone," said Grammy. "We can call it Mindfulness Day. We'll do other things. Okay?"

Addie lowered her head, doubtfully. She wasn't sure she wanted to be *that* mindful.

"C'mon, it'll be fun," said Grammy, giving her a nudge. "Let's go meet the new chickens. You can name them!"

Addie forgot about texting or playing on her tablet when she saw the two new Rhode Island Reds.

"Cluck, cluck, cluck, cluck... CLUCKAAAAAWWWK!" the chickens called.

Maude made a mad dash, sliding on a rug up to the screen door. She looked on, happily, as the chickens pecked at the ground.

"Grammy, they're beautiful!" Addie exclaimed. "I wanna hold them. C'mon— let's go outside! You come, too, Maudie. But no chasing."

Grammy, Maude, and Addie walked into a small courtyard where the chickens were strutting around. At first, Maude tried to sniff them, but chickens don't like dog sniffs. Finally, Maude lay down in the grassy yard and watched as Grammy taught Addie how to pick them up.

"Be gentle, Adalyn Grace. I know you love animals, but they may be a little afraid."

Addie picked up the smallest hen and sat down with her on a garden bench, stroking her silky feathers. "Grammy, her feathers are s-o-o-o soft! I wanna name her Ruby Red."

Grammy sat down beside Addie, holding the other Rhode Island Red, and Maude crept close enough to put her nose on the bird's tail.

Addie reached over to pet the second hen, perched peacefully on Grammy's lap. "I can feel her breathing. Her heart is beating right under my hand," Addie whispered. "She's so sweet. Let's name her Red Velvet!"

Addie and Grammy sat close together on the bench enjoying the chickens, sunshine, and mid-morning sounds. Then Maude tried to edge in between Addie and Grammy on the bench, wanting to be included.

"Look! Maude's trying to make friends with the chickens," said Addie.

"The five of us are bonding," Grammy replied.

"What's that?"

"It means becoming close. Even pets can be a close part of the family."

"Maudie, you're the best dog in the whole wide world!" said Addie, stroking her friend's head. "Don't be jealous of the chickens—they'll never replace you! We've got lots of love to go around."

Grammy gave Maude a pat, too, and told Addie to listen to the sweet sounds the chickens were making.

"It's like they're talking to us," said Addie.

"I think they're happy to meet you."

"Woof!" said Maude with a bark of approval.

"Let's clean up from breakfast and put the chickens back in their pen now, Addie. We want them to be safe while we're at the lake."

"Okay Grammy. *Sit*, Maude. *Stay*, while we put the chickens away."

Back indoors, Addie noticed that the kitchen still smelled like pancakes and syrup. She walked to the sink and decided to do the dishes. Sudsy dishwater felt slick in the sink, and maple syrup was stuck to the plates.

"Grammy, the syrup's so sticky. I can feel it under my fingers."

"Just rinse it off with warm water," Grammy said.

"Okay, now the dishes aren't sticky; they're slippery."

Addie looked at each plate carefully before loading it into the dishwasher. Grammy packed a bag and Maude paced around the kitchen, ready for her favorite part of the day—walking to the lake! She trotted to the back door, wagging her fluffy tail.

"You're such a wiggle butt, Maude." Addie giggled, clicking the leash on Maude's collar.

"Come on Addie, let's leave the phone at home," Grammy added kindly, slipping a sparkly, pink cell phone out of Addie's back pocket and placing it on the kitchen table.

"This is Mindfulness Day, so it's important that we notice what we see and hear and smell on our walk," explained Grammy as they strolled to the lake. "What do you notice right now, Addie?"

Addie stood still. "The air smells like pine, and I just heard a pine cone drop. I smell honeysuckle. And I can hear splashy sounds—I think people are paddling canoes and kayaks in the lake," said Addie. "Everybody sounds happy."

While Grammy talked with friends, Addie and Maude walked down to the water. Maude pulled on her long leash, chasing some squawking ducks into the water, and Addie walked barefoot for a while in the sand. Then she sat down, very still, turning her face to the sun.

"How does the sunshine feel on your face?" Maude asked quietly, lying down beside her friend and catching her breath.

"It's bright and warm and kind of tingly on my skin," Addie said. "It gets hot, but when I turn away, it gets cool again. And when I open my eyes, everything looks a little different. The clouds seem puffier, like big marshmallows. And the sky is bright blue—like the icing on my birthday cake."

Addie thought for a moment. "Is this bonding, Maude, since we're doing mindfulness and sharing a special day together?"

"Yes, sweet girl."

"Then I think Mindfulness Day is my favorite."

Addie smiled. Then she stood up and brushed the sand off her shorts. "Come on, Maude," she giggled. "Race you to the dock!"

Grammy, Maude, and Addie spent their morning at the lake, watching canoes glide through the water, turtles sunbathe on logs, and little gray-blue herons wade in the shallows. "Look up, Addie," said Grammy, as they strolled around the lake.

They stopped to admire a pair of red-tailed hawks with streaked bellies and cinnamon-red tails flying higher and higher, making spirals in the summer sky. And Addie watched, not taking her eyes off the hawks for a long, long time.

Just being mindful.

These questions are intended for parents, teachers, and other caregivers to encourage children to discuss the material in the book and to further develop interactional moments for the readers.

1. Why did Addie and Maude wake up in the middle of the night? How did Addie and Maude react?

2. What number did Addie count to with her breaths when Maude was teaching Addie mindful breathing? Why do you think Maude wanted Addie to count her in breaths and out breaths?

3. What makes visiting her grandmother special for Addie? How does a day at her Grammy's differ from her days at home?

4. What kinds of pancakes did Grammy make? How does eating breakfast become a mindful moment for Addie?

5. What flowers make Addie sneeze? Why did Maude want Addie to think about how things look or smell?

6. What did the hand soap smell like? What is important about Addie noticing the scent of the soap?

7. What did Grammy call their day without a phone or a computer or a tablet? What is important about that kind of day? Why do you think Grammy placed Addie's phone on the kitchen table?

8. How many new chickens did Grammy have in her backyard? What did Addie name the chickens? Why do you think she chose those names?

9. What was making splashy sounds at the lake? Describe what Addie and Maude might look like in a kayak or a canoe. Would Grammy need to be with them to do this?

10. Where in your body do you feel bonding with someone or something you love? When do you feel that closeness? What things could you do to create bonding moments in your life?

This book is dedicated to teaching mindfulness practices to children and those who care for them. These practices include both sensory awareness and emotional bonding. Developing skills to combat life's challenges may begin as early as infancy. I hope you will savor the tiny moments that Maude, my Australian Shepherd, creates for you as you read this book.

The real-life Maude was my faithful companion for more than fifteen years. She taught me about devotion, forgiveness, and patience. And her constant love and support—to me and to my many therapy clients—touched me in the deepest parts of my heart and soul. She held me up through death, divorce, a stroke, and even brain surgery.

Maude demonstrated great caring for my patients, particularly those who saw her as a source of strength and courage. She accepted all emotions without judgment and soothed many during tough therapy sessions. She attended mindfulness therapy and even alerted us once during a group meeting that someone was having a low blood sugar attack!

Maude, like other dogs, lived in the moment. These loyal companions live for our love and attention. They also live to give love and comfort to others in times of joy, sorrow, sickness, or social distancing.

Sometimes young people will listen to animals before humans, and so Maude became the mindfulness teacher in this book. My hope is that she will help young readers slow down to notice the present—something that is at the core of mindfulness practice—and to put down their electronics in favor of pockets of time for bonding and connecting with each other.

Much love and gratitude to all of my patients and mindfulness students who inspired me to create this book. To my inspirational editor, Peggy Shaw, I owe great appreciation. To my family: Kirstin, Madi, and Drew Kochanek, and Dennis Manske, thank you for your love and commitment during this process. And thank you to everyone at Mascot Books for believing in this project!

—Pamela Cappetta, EdD